A place for PLUTO

D0178502

written by STEF WADE
illustrated by MELANIE DEMMER

Raintree is an imprint of Capstone Global Library Limited, a company incorporated in England and Wales having its registered office at 264 Banbury Road, Oxford, OX2 7DY – Registered company number: 6695582

www.raintree.co.uk
myorders@raintree.co.uk

Designed by Aruna Rangarajan
Original illustrations © Capstone Global Library Limited 2019
Originated by Capstone Global Library Ltd
Printed and bound in India

ISBN 978 1 4747 6327 1
22 21 20 19 18
10 9 8 7 6 5 4 3 2 1

British Library Cataloguing in Publication Data
A full catalogue record for this book is available from the British Library.

For the better part of forever, Pluto was a planet. One of the

FAMOUS NINE.

MARS

MERCURY

EARTH

VENUS

He was the smallest and the furthest from the Sun, but he was proud to be a planet just the same.

PLUTO

SATURN

NEPTUNE

JUPITER

URANUS

Even though Pluto orbited around the Sun and was mostly round, the creatures on Earth decided he was

TOO SMALL.

Pluto was
CRUSHED.

He tried to
PROTEST.

#PLUTOBELONGS

NOT

FAIR

STAND

WITH

PLUTO

But it was **NO USE.**

There,
there.

Feeling sad and rejected, Pluto left with Charon and his other four moons by his side to find his place in the galaxy.

As Pluto moved along, his friend
Halley's Comet streaked past.

Haven't seen
you in a while!

Yeah, I get that a lot.

Halley was a comet and still a part of the solar system. But comets have tails, and Pluto did not.

Pluto wasn't a comet or a planet.
HE WAS A NOBODY.

Feeling more blue **than** brown,
Pluto kept moving.

When Pluto saw Gem, Persi and Ori crashing in as dusty, rocky comet tails, he wondered if he could join them.

Then Ida the asteroid came by. Pluto and Ida were nearly the same size. Pluto thought he'd finally figured out his true identity.

Pluto wasn't a planet
or a comet or an asteroid.
He missed being a planet.
He missed his old friends.

HE MISSED FEELING LIKE HE BELONGED.

He spun around the Sun like
everyone else, but he wasn't
a planet or a comet or an
asteroid or a meteoroid.

Pluto had nowhere to turn. He was about to give up when he saw someone he'd never seen before. He felt like he was **LOOKING IN A MIRROR!**

Pardon me if I sound rude, but what are you?

Pluto stared in wonder at the four dwarf planets. They were too small to be planets but too big to be rocks. They were not planets or comets or asteroids or meteoroids. They were

JUST LIKE HIM!

Pluto felt more like himself than ever before. He couldn't wait to tell his old friends about his new ones. Turns out his old friends missed him too!

We're sorry, Pluto!
we ♥ Pluto
Just because you're not a planet any more doesn't mean we don't love you!

Pluto was over the moon. He was a part of the solar system, with friends both old and new. He smiled an intergalactic smile that was out of this Milky Way.

WHAT'S THE DEAL WITH PLUTO?

In 1930, Pluto was discovered as the ninth planet in the solar system.

I made it! Awesome!

In 2006, Pluto was told he was not a planet any more.

Oh no!

POOR PLUTO! WHY?

Scientists decided that to be a planet, it must:

- orbit around the Sun ✓

- have a round shape ✓

- be able to clear its own orbit by pulling asteroids towards itself, making the asteroids part of the planet.

This bit could be tricky for me!

Pluto does orbit around the Sun and is mostly round. But Pluto is small (only half the size of the United States) and shares the area around its orbit with Neptune and many other large objects in an area called the Kuiper Belt.

BFFs!

But Pluto isn't alone. Other dwarf planets such as Ceres, Eris, Haumea and Makemake cannot clear an object out of their paths either.